MIKE'S TRIP TO UTOPIA

MIKE'S TRIP TO UTOPIA

A VERY FUNNY BOOK

BY BARNABY HASLAM

This edition published in 2023
by Maida Vale Publishing,
An imprint of The Black Spring Press Group,
London, United Kingdom

Cover design by Barnaby Haslam
Typeset by Subash Raghu

ISBN 978-1-915406-29-3

www.blackspringpressgroup.com

CHAPTER 1: HISTORY

Fathoming the countless days
That history seems to share,
We realise that our dear names
Are neither here nor there.

Cultivate your garden, man,
The best is yet to come.
Thank the helpful market man
For his is not undone.

Mine is worth its weight in gold,
In treason, lust or want.
Save me till I'm ill and old
Because life's just a hunt.

To tell you about Mike's pre-life I need to tell you
how he was born. To tell you that, I need to tell you
about his father. It all started with the Fool. The Fool
was a large, square building that emerged fully formed
in an area remote from the city. Its walls were smooth
and grey with a dozen windows and a large doorway
at the front.

Paddy, Mike's father, was the Fool who existed first. He took residence in the large, square building but began to feel lonely. He became less foolish and built a new building next to his and called it Manners. It, too, was large and grey with twelve windows.

Over time, the two buildings became inhabited by a diverse range of things and beings, some of them developing into human beings.

Paddy moved into Manners and began a love affair with a woman from Fool called Janice. Now living in different buildings, together they decided to make a home for themselves in a new house between Fool and Manners. They called it Silly. They had many children, most of them boys, but also some girls. Their last child, a boy, they named Mike.

CHAPTER 2: YOUTH

Can you remember being innocent?
When roundness was the score?
Does memory itself deny repent?
And can we have some more?

Perhaps you've never lost the charm
Of gainsay loving openness.
Enthusiasm doesn't harm,
Yet sinless isn't painless.

What the sin that makes us sad?
What the chance for glee?
What the time when I was mad?
Ambivalently me.

Mike's early life was quiet. He went to school and did all the usual things. Although a rather quiet child, he had enough friends to keep him happy.

When Mike was fifteen, he was invited to a river-boat party in the summer. This was his first outing at a party without his parents. It was his first taste of independence.

It was a sunny day and around ten girls and boys left the river bank with food and drink for the afternoon and began to enjoy themselves. A taste of freedom. Mike was wearing new clothes; everyone looked good. There was laughter, embarrassment, talk, awkwardness, good humour and organisation.

What power Mike felt! He discovered a new confidence. He realised he could make people laugh. In the girls he discovered a beauty completely new to him. A beauty that enclosed and dissipated. It comforted and dared equally. Challenged and nourished him.

"I see the meaning of the world," he said. "This is the infinite." He had fallen in love with romance and had no control over it.

That night, after he'd got back, he was in his pyjamas and brushing his teeth. He looked at himself in the mirror. His reflection moved in a different way. Mike raised his left arm but his reflection didn't. He scowled. The reflection smiled.

The reflection began to talk.

"Do you know how many palimpsests there are in your irises?"

"No," said Mike.

"Forty-two."

"What's a palimpsest?"

"It's when you get restless in the night and have to change positions and sleep with your head on the pillow, sometimes on the left side, sometimes on the right. And it doesn't matter how restless you get in a night, you can always change sides," said his reflection.

"And that's happening in my eyes?"

"Yes."

"But how do you know?" said Mike.

"OK. Look into my eyes."

"I am."

"Right. How many colours can you see?"

"One," said Mike.

"Now," said the reflection, "divide that colour into forty-two.."

"OK" said Mike.

"Done that? Right, now count why it wouldn't be difficult to take all the different patterns you can see and make them into one object."

"You're making me very tired."

"That's how it works!"

"But you could spend hours doing that," said Mike.

"You could spend an eternity doing that!"

Mike laughed. The reflection laughed. They laughed out loud.

Mike jolted and felt a strong breeze and daylight on his body. Still in his pyjamas, he discovered he was standing on top of a large, flat-roofed building, overlooking a sort of campus. In front of him was enormous red lettering, a meter high, spelling out the word MANNERS, back to front, so anyone looking up at the building could see it.

He felt a remarkable athleticism about his being. His eyesight was keen and he felt proud and vividly alive. He must move, explore. He began to look around and noticed a trap door near where he stood.

CHAPTER 3: MANNERS

Destiny or random fate
Are often met at odds.
It thrives on how you can relate
To chosen friendly bods.

I do not know what paths there are,
In fact it's up to me
To find my perfect golfing par
And see what I can be.

Truth will follow, if I'm true,
I may uncover more.
Reading time is spotless, new
And writing sets the score.

Standing high on the roof of Manners, Mike saw ahead
of him a huge road with buildings either side. In the distance he could make out a coastline: a sort of shipyard.
In the mid-distance he saw many buildings of varying
sizes; further away was grassland and to the left he saw
an expanse of countryside surrounded by hills.

He climbed down through the trap door and down a step-ladder. Inside was a corridor with doors down each side. Coming from one of the doors was the voice of a woman telling a story. He listened.

"There was a woman. Day and night she travelled along the track until she was so exhausted she had to stop and find somewhere to stay. During the night she dreamt of falling off a high bank and landing on a mountain of fabrics, all of bright colour and design. When the hat she was wearing leapt off her head and ran off down the side of the mountain, she froze and stared up at the sky. She saw a giant horse which she climbed on to but because the horse was so big and scary she woke up in a cold sweat. When she looked in the mirror in the morning she couldn't see the reflection of herself. Vanished. And no one saw her ever again."

"That was very boring," came the voice of a small boy.

Mike wandered along the corridor and came across a woman in a white dress. Her grey hair was pulled back by a black hair band. She walked lightly towards Mike.

"Morning," she said.

She introduced herself as Whistle and led Mike into another of the side rooms. Inside was a single bed with a young man in it. Beside the bed was a cabinet with a glass of water. The young man stared upwards with an absentness in his look, his dark hair combed neatly. Sunlight poured in from a tall window with white drapes. The ceiling was high and the room simple and clean. Whistle and Mike pulled up wooden chairs.

"This is the School of Manners," she explained. "It is a place for gifted people and for helping the disabled. We are in a place called Hero. It's like a village. It has everything you need. You could meet God, go to Slime House, The Ol'factory, Commuting, the Coast, Outdoors, The Theatre, The Mall, Bells and meet some of the Guardians."

Mike didn't know what to say. One minute he was brushing his teeth, the next, he was talking to a woman called Whistle in a place called Hero.

"What's going on?" he said.

"Everyone is born with a hunger. A need. A desire. Hero is designed specifically to help meet those needs. This hunger," she explained, "can be infinite, unnameable, demonic, divine and human. Hero is here to help you. Until you satisfy yourself you will not suffer. It's best to have a thirst for knowledge, and to fulfil your desires until you feel satisfied. When that moment comes, a Guardian will know. You will then start the rest of your life, which will contain suffering. This is your chance."

A whole vista of possibilities occurred to Mike. Did he need to feel guilty? Certainly not!

Mike listened, trying not to be put off by the quiet eeriness of the invalid beside them.

"We all start life in Eyes," she said. "Eyes is the world of ideas, language and thought and it is infinite. Every dream, word, thought, emotion and idea exists in the world of Eyes. To get there all you have to do is yawn. To get back to Hero all you have to do is giggle. It will always be with you.

"Guardians help run Hero. When one of them makes a mistake, someone in Hero, it could be you, goes up to Eyes. When someone has made it in Hero, fulfilled themselves, a Guardian connected to that person will ding a little cowbell, and your life in reality will begin then.

"Guardians have fulfilled themselves but can stay on in Hero to help organise it and maintain it. Ed is in charge of education. Phil is in charge of philosophy. Moray is in charge of morality. Other Guardians are Dom domesticity, Gen geniality, Beliefs, Reason and the Busses.

"The female Guardians combine light and dark qualities. Miss Understood. Miss Me. Miss Adventure. Miss Judge. Miss Nomer and others. Most of them like a drink.

The nature of your stay in Hero defines your future character," she said.

It turned out that no one knew as much about Hero as Whistle, and she didn't let on to Mike that she was his mother, Janice being her real name. He didn't recognised her.

Paddy, Mike's father, and Janice had moved out of Silly due to a heavy workload and moments of extreme silliness. Janice, now Whistle, lived in the School of Manners and Paddy, a patron of the School of the Fool, next door, lived in the countryside growing vegetables and keeping rabbits.

Mike was trying to take all this in.

In the School of Manners were many rooms dedicated to learning and teaching; people of all ages with books, toys, musical instruments, gadgets, balls and scientific apparatus. A school for the gifted. Next door was the School of the Fool.

"What's the School of the Fool?" said Mike.

"For those who require nothing but have gained everything," Whistle explained. "But they are Guardians nonetheless and can leave at any time."

Mike and Whistle moved downstairs. The main room was large, containing vast bookshelves, desks and a grand piano. A young man was thrashing away at the piano keys, which made no sound whatsoever. Next to him was a woman dressed in tweed doing a hip-hop style dance. In the corner were two men singing to each other and a man sat at a desk reading poetry.

A tall man walked in through the front door.

"Perfect timing, Ed!" said Whistle. "Ed can show you round the School of the Fool," she said to Mike.

Ed and Mike introduced themselves. Whistle made her farewells, saying she had to go upstairs to tend to the young man and Ed and Mike left through the main door and stood outside. It was bright outside; a clock chimed one. They crossed the gravel, past Silly, from where they heard the sound of jaunty classical music and the scraping of chair legs on the floor.

Ed told Mike to prepare himself. The Fools inside were wise but not necessarily understandable to other people. They approached the main door then walked in.

CHAPTER 4: FOOL

The clown expels the very fear
Which gives him might and time.
His flaws of talent bring what's clear
To surface in his mime.

With no such concept as a mind
He transcends culture's norm.
Inhabiting a nameless kind,
A bravery of form.

In states like this his act is made,
To please and show his trust.
And when it's done respects are paid,
For end it should and must.

The main room of The School of The Fool, which was
the whole of the ground floor, contained an empty
swimming pool, the ceiling was high and everything
looked old and decayed. There was an assortment of
metal staircases around the walls, where damp patches
were revealed between areas of tiling, most of which
had fallen to the floor. There was a strong damp smell

and shrieks and moans could be heard from various directions.

Suspended in mid-air above the swimming pool, at a diagonal angle, head down, feet up, her body straight and rigid, was an elderly woman in a bathing costume and bathing hat. She was having an almost meaning-less conversation with another Fool who was standing near the edge of the pool. He was extremely tall, wore an old pair of boxer shorts and had a wide ruff around his neck. His body was pale and thin and there was a sad, lonely look on his face. He pleaded with the sus-pended woman who was shouting back at him, giving him all sorts of advice.

Dandelion Fool: "If I could just be a croquet hoop I could..." He looked at her pleadingly.

Woman: "You can be, darling. You just have to think it."

Dandelion Fool: "If four. Hang on. If four. Wait. I said if four knew how not to stay on the ground it would probably have feathers." (He smiles.) "Add three to a Fool no more astute than 700 wigs in a line, all of them shouting, 'Alive!' But no, she said, and wisely, for they will never be able to count long with their tongues in their mouths, shrieking, for counting doesn't help me." (He smiles.)

Ed and Mike left the pool Fools and went through a large doorway by the side of the pool, which led to a staircase where they went to see some other Fools, who were living in cell-like chambers on a corridor upstairs. The noise of the swimming pool Fools had faded; so had the damp smell. Now, Mike could hear different sounds coming from the cells. It was warmer up here and there were the scents of candles and incense.

The first cell they came to contained many cushions and drapes and a man sitting on a rug in the centre of the floor, smoking a pipe. The room was full of fabrics, rugs, hangings, incense sticks, candles, beads, sculptures, bells, mugs and ropes. The Fool's hair was long, dark and matted; coins, string and braids woven into the thick strands. His coat and trousers were multi-coloured; he muttered gently and fast to himself in short sentences, mottoes, anecdotes, quotations and facts. His speech was soft and quick and came out in little utterances. He noticed Ed and Mike as they looked in and gave them a little smile. The Fool was quite calm and the sun was shining through the window, casting beams of smoke-filled light on to the rug, lighting up beads and other bits on the floor.

The next cell was empty save for the top hatted Fool inside. He had a pig's bladder slung around his neck and his coat was long and dark. He also smiled as they walked by.

The next Fool they saw was a tall bald man sitting down at a desk with a pen and paper. The sun shone in this room too and the Fool seemed to radiate a light and heat all of his own. He was writing, his large hand mastering the thin pen on the page. Like the others before him, he smiled as they looked in.

Turning to another corridor, they saw seven short men, all wearing pale grey suits and ties, performing a dance together. It took place at the opposite end of the corridor from Ed and Mike and from a distance, it appeared as though the Seven Suited Fools were experiencing a higher degree of gravity than is usually expected. Their dance involved much leaping. On the spot but also off walls and including many frog leaps, landing speedily, as if in an upwardly moving elevator. The dance, which was highly amusing to watch, took a few minutes. All the Seven Suited Fools' faces were entirely neutral, despite the vigorous athleticism of their dance. Not even their ties flapped about. They were all immaculately dressed, with black shoes, and looked at Ed and Mike throughout the whole routine. Ed and Mike were transfixed for a few minutes.

The dance finished and everyone moved on; the dancers in various directions, Ed and Mike down another staircase and finally to a small exit at the front of The School of The Fool.

"We've only seen the merest surface of this building," said Ed, looking at Mike.

"Really?" Mike said. He couldn't imagine how many Fools there could be. As he spoke, a beautiful woman walked past. She was wearing a bright red bikini and was drinking from a small black bottle.

"Morning," she said as she walked past. Ed looked at Mike and raised his eyebrows.

They had come to the door at the far right side of the building and walked round to the front, just outside Silly.

"How would you like to meet the happiest couple in Hero?" said Ed.

Mike said he would love to.

"We'll find them in Silly," said Ed.

So that's where they went.

CHAPTER 5: SILLY

The conscience of the hourglass
Has much it wants to say,
Like "How do you do?" and "What a farce!"
And "How do you spend your day?"

Accustomed to the light by now,
We fall into our place.
The hills are breathing, cats meow
And on with the old race.

The time will come to see it through,
To die in peace with wraith,
Forever after being true
To God and love and faith.

Ed walked up to Silly and knocked on the door. It opened and they were faced by a smiley man in a check shirt and jeans who introduced himself as Tony and welcomed them in. Inside was a smiley-faced woman who stood up and introduced herself as Sarah. Sarah'n'Tony liked to make people feel welcome.

The room was small, a wooden table with an orange and blue tablecloth in the centre and around the walls were a dozen framed watercolour paintings, which Tony said he had painted himself. There was a wooden dresser and on the right was an enamel stove with a kettle bobbling away on top.

"Tea?" said Tony, looking around at everyone. Everyone said "Yes, please," and things got going.

"Is the sugar in the Daft, Sarah?" said Tony. He liked to call the cupboard "Daft" because he kept forgetting where things were kept and felt a fool when he couldn't remember.

Ed knew them well and had been round for tea many times. As Sarah'n'Tony were the happiest couple in Hero, they lived in Silly, right between the School of Manners and the School of the Fool.

They all talked about Hero and what there was to do. One particular subject they covered was a place called "More Like A Room", or "MLAR". Tony explained to Mike it was beyond the Mall and Commuting but not as far away as Bells. He explained that it was an eight-sided building with one side left open.

"If you want to express yourself, but cannot think of anywhere else in Hero you could do that, you must go to MLAR. Hero has many things, but it can't cater for every single emotion. Sarah'n'I did well, we didn't need to go there. The mind is more complicated than its surroundings. The mind is also more flawed than its surroundings. If you feel you need to talk to someone, if you feel the need to escape, to say whatever you want, then go to MLAR."

Mike said he understood and that he had begun to write poems. Short, three verse ballads.

There was a knock on the side door and the sound of bubbling and gurgling. Tony let in a tall man whose head was enclosed in a cuboid fish tank. Inside the tank, bubbles fell noisily upwards from his mouth as he spoke. The water was milky and weedy and the man's large blue eyes could be seen. The side door led directly to the School of Manners.

"Would you like some tea, Bottle?" said Sarah. Bottle smiled and gurgled so Sarah poured some tea into the top of the tank. Bottle was a Guardian but never went to the Guardian's Ball. He did once. "We can hear exactly what you're saying, Bottle. And it's not nice." He had certain functions of a legislative and legal nature.

There was another noise coming from the other side of the kitchen. (The door that lead to the School of the Fool.) "I just want to put up this notice!" shouted a Fool from behind the door.

"It's Nuncle," said Tony. Nuncle had a notice that he wanted to pin to the other side of the door. It read, "Wanted: Clown. Riddles. Magic. Loon."

Nuncle had put up his notice and started laughing and shouting in a maddening way. Tony opened the side door and said loudly and politely, "Will you shut the fuck up?!"

When Tony had said the word "fuck", Sarah had coincidentally and loudly scraped her chair backwards, making a noise that covered up the word "fuck".

"Oh, sorry," said Nuncle, and looned off into the building.

Nuncle had had many songs written about him. He had an interesting past but consistently denied it.

It began to rain outside and the water ran down the two windows. It was warm inside and everyone felt cosy.

"I think you should go to the Mall this afternoon", Ed said to Mike. "Perhaps you'll meet someone and go to Slime House! Or you could go to the coast and meet God."

"What's God like?", said Mike.

"He's a big, bald, fat old man. But he's very kind. If a touch irritable."

They cleared up the tea things and Tony showed everyone his watercolours. Sarah put on some classical music and they all had a weird dance for a minute. Ed said that he would show Mike to the Mall, so after saying bye to Bottle and Sarah'n'Tony, they left.

The rain had stopped and beyond the distant buildings was a beautiful rainbow. A meteor was flying overhead: a burning ball of rock, diminishing in size and gradually falling, heading away from Ed and Mike to where Ed said the coast was. Off they walked towards the Mall.

CHAPTER 6: TOWN

Currents of the whirligig
Occur to cultured men.
From why we wear the leaves of fig
To egg came first or hen.

Artists of the past we know
Have stimulating force,
To influence the way we grow
And make us say "of course".

Do you want an influence
To help the world to thrive?
Direct the local confluence
And keep the world alive?

Mike was taken to the Mall by Ed where he left him to explore on his own. The Mall was a large nave with stalls and entertainments down each side on three storeys with a huge spiral staircase at the far end. The roof was glass. The nature of Mike's first visit to the Mall was sequential, visiting one establishment after another.

TECHNOLOGY AND FASHION. Mike discovered some great trends and ideas that would sustain him.

THE EARWAX EMPORIUM was on the ground floor near the entrance to the Mall. It had a large glass façade with large automatically-opening glass doors. The floor inside was tiled with hard, cold, mustard coloured tiles. Was it cold in there because of the air conditioning? The room was large and there was a persistent hum coming from a large white box on the ceiling. A man and a woman, looking like air stewards, stood behind a reception desk. Mike walked in and sat down on a huge leather, mustard coloured, puffy sofa and looked at the thin plant potted next to it. A man came out with an electric floor polisher and began sweeping it about. The room smelt of wax. He noticed another man and a woman sitting on a darker, puffy sofa. They were picking their ears then inspecting their fingers and putting the gooey leftovers in their mouths. He began to pick his own ears and eat it. He did this for some minutes, lulled by the humming noise and shiny mustardyness of it all.

NOISY TOUCHY THINGS was not far away. The first thing he did was unwrap a xylophone from orange cellophane. The floor was green and rubbery. The whole thing collapsed before he could completely unwrap it and the keys fell everywhere, bouncing and clunking.

THETH was a department store where everything inside was made from human hair. Desks, curtains, wallpaper, lamps, coffee sets. The carpet was extremely thick, so everyone moved around noiselessly. In exchange for having your hair cut you could get a free pair of corduroy trousers.

FLAVOURLESS FOOD advertised mashed seagull, served only between 1am and 5am.

FEATHERS INK was dedicated to all the pleasures to be had from feathers. And ink.

SOFT SHEETS AND PILLOWS was next door to FEATHERS INK.

HO HO HO. This was a room with many single wooden desks with chairs. At the far end was a work surface next to which stood a Guardian. He had some large red ear defenders which he gave to people who came in. On this occasion Mike was the only person in there. He went in and was given a pair of the red ear defenders. He could hear nothing. Just silence. There were some ambiguous posters on the walls.

Just then, very clearly, he heard an "ahem", the sound of a man gently clearing his throat. The ear defenders were actually sound-proof headphones. Pause. What followed was a collection of different throat clearings. Some coughing too. Each one had a pause before and after it. Some were gentle, some serious. This continued for a few minutes, each "ahem" and cough surprising Mike. After some more of this, Mike burst out laughing. A kind of blankness overwhelmingly needing to be filled. He looked down and saw some rude graffiti on the desk. He stopped laughing. Another cough. He left.

ITCH BENEFITS was where you could have your shins scratched.

THE SCHOOL OF GENUINE ASTONISHMENT. Mike found himself in a largish room where there was a group of men and women sitting on chairs in a circle, each with a script on their lap. As he walked in, they all seemed to be doing a "one potata, two potata, three potata" routine but as Mike set eyes on them they began reading from their scripts.

Woman: "You've heard about the Ball?"
Man: "Yes."
Woman: " You must find someone to go to it with."
Man: "Why's that?"
Woman: "It helps if you've got someone else."
Man: "I see."
Woman: "Find someone to go to the Ball with and you'll be fine."
Mike blinked and paused. They hadn't seen him, but when he started to walk away they resumed their "One potata, two potata, three potata" game.

HYPOTHETICAL GAMBLING: Buying shares in someone's personality using your own personality. Glee and excitement. A bookmaker cum disco. Dancing at the kiosk.

THAT'S EXACTLY WHAT I WANTED TO HEAR. This was a restaurant. Mike was led to a table and given a napkin and a glass of wine. He relaxed and began to hear seafaring noises; the tightening of rope, gulls and ferry accompaniment, as well as breezes.

A woman came up to the table. Her footsteps sounded like meows. He got up to meet her but when he spoke, he didn't recognise the sound that came out. It sounded pleasant and it sounded English but he didn't recognise any of the words that came out. The woman spoke in the same abstract way as he did and he understood her. They ate together and throughout the whole meal they spoke in this gobbledygook sounding way. His hand temporarily turned into a metal piston, nearly knocking over the vase with the flower. Her hands temporarily grew olive leaves as they spoke. There were no pass walkers during intimacies. Other eaters tended to be spilling milk from small jugs.

The room was tall and airy with white drapes by the windows. When she did up the buttons on her cardigan, they made a loud popping sound. Things flowed well in the ambience of the meal. Certainly she was an attractive girl.

Later, they went to the theatre.

THE FART DANCE. At the door of the theatre they were given stylish gas masks to wear during the performance. The theatre company was called 'Lamp Men and the Jadeless Mortals'. Opening the performance was a clown who declared the following:

"Herald.
Moon come round.
Twice fold.
Jadeless mortals.
Lamp men and scowls.
Schildren und peeves.
Bog roots and holes.
Sac heap.
Moulds.
Scup."
Then the Fart Dance began. It was a ballet of farting.
During the interval, the audience could take off their
gas masks and enjoy their own smells. At the end of
the show each performer was lifted from the stage ver-
tically by invisible chords.

It was pleasant afterwards walking down the avenue
of Hero. However, Mike and the woman decided not
to meet up again.

CHAPTER 7: THE GUYS

Macro worries plague the set
To tell us all what's wrong.
I wonder if it's up to me
To scream or hit the gong.

TV's comfort slices worry,
Freeing us from guilt.
Healing with morality,
Clothing us in felt.

Vote and hold it really tight,
Read the paper, too.
Put up the good ruddy fight,
You know I love you too.

A new day and elsewhere in Hero some of the male
Guardians went for a picnic.

The Guys:

Phil	Philosophy, tall and wiry
Ed	Education, ballsy and friendly
Reason	Reliable, scruffy
Gen	Geniality
Dom	Domesticity
Moray	Morality, an all rounder
Beliefs	Quiet

They go on a car journey to the countryside.

ED
What are you doing, Phil?
PHIL
I'm just checking we've got some spare fuel.
ED
Is the rug in there too?
PHIL
Yeah, it should be OK.
ED
The nozzle's not going to leak is it?
PHIL
No. It's alright, it's got one of those washer things on it.

ED

I just don't want any fuel getting on the rug.

PHIL

Have you got the sandwiches?

ED

Yup.

BELIEFS

Hey. I was wondering if you could come and look at these seatbelts. I mean, it just seems they're a bit loose. They told me…

MORAY

Guys, can we hurry up please? It looks like it's going to rain. I don't want to spend the next half an hour waiting for you lot to get ready.

ED

It doesn't matter about the fuel for the moment.

DOM

What? I'll put the cups in the basket.

MORAY

Yeah, that's fine.

PHIL

You two are never going to fit into the back seat. There's Moray and Nick already. There won't be enough room.

DOM

Who's going in the front?

ED

I am.

MORAY

Actually, Nick's not coming.

PHIL

Why, where is he?

MORAY

He's down the Ol'factory.

DOM

It's alright, Gen and I are going to merge anyway.

GEN

Hi.

(GEN walks into DOM as if a ghost and they merge into the appearance of DOM. All the others seem to experience the air around them.)

DOM

Are you gonna drive?

BELIEFS

Yes.

(They all get into the car, put seatbelts on and set off.)

ED

How long 'til the road hits that turning?

MORAY

Did you know, Phil, that out of all the different species of animals, only one has the ability to make a reed bed into an actual platform for something?

PHIL

What do you mean?

MORAY

I mean that the field lizard can make a hundred foot wigs in a week but it can't actually leap into the air without a platform because there are so few hatches.

PHIL

Carry on.

MORAY

Yes. By the time a field lizard can mate, it can only swim for half a kilometre in either direction. So by the time the foot wigs have replaced themselves with natural growth, it's taken too long for the journey to have been worth it in the first place, so it has to use a reed bed.

DOM

Are you talking about sex again?

BELIEFS

Could you pass Ed the map, Dom.

MORAY

Yes, but in a world where all the lizards were able to fly, you'd expect that some of them would actually stop needing foot wigs. Unless there was a different reason for them.

PHIL

But that would depend on the climate, surely?

ED

Seeing as lizards are cold-blooded anyway would mean that none of the scales would have evolved enough by that time anyway.

(Everyone is pleased for the moment as the journey continues.)

MORAY

Pass us that cowbell will you, Dom.

(MORAY dings the cowbell and someone in Hero leaves.)

DOM

We are going to have a damn fine picnic.

BELIEFS

We are completely lost.

ED

Drive on a bit.

(They carry on driving until BELIEFS, the driver, pulls the vehicle over to a lay-by and gets out. Another man who was on a bicycle by the side of the road gets into the driver's seat and takes over the driving. He has BELIEFS printed in white on the back of his black jacket as well. The first BELIEFS is left behind with the bike.

Meanwhile, as Mike is having a doze elsewhere, he dreams he is being chased through a city by men in grey suits.)

ED
Yeah, Phil. Beliefs was saying he put that CD on but couldn't hear it because he said it was so good.

PHIL
Couldn't hear it because it was so good?

ED
Yeah. That's what you said wasn't it, Beliefs?

BELIEFS
Yeah, but I heard it yesterday and it rocks.

PHIL
Ed, can you move your chair forward a bit?

DOM
You said that Nick got it for you.

BELIEFS
Yeah. He got it off one of his mates down the Ol'factory.

ED
Cool

DOM
It's very weird. Every decent single that Tan brings out, nobody's heard of it.

ED
It's not that weird.

BELIEFS
What do you mean, "not weird"?

PHIL
Shut up, Beliefs.

MORAY
I'm just saying that it's pretty weird that every time nobody hears of a Tan single, somebody decent gets it out. It's disgusting.

DOM
It was me actually, Moray. I was telling everyone...

PHIL
I was listening.

ED
You've never even heard of Tan.

MORAY
I have, actually.

(Suddenly, from behind the back seat...)

REASON

Bollocks!

MORAY

Ah, there you are, Reason.

PHIL

Oh my God, Reason, it's you.

REASON

Yes.

PHIL

How's the disease?

REASON

Yes. S'alright. Not bad.

(ED turns round quickly and bangs his elbow on the door. Someone in Hero goes back to EYES)

MORAY

I think Phil's got that CD if you want to put it on, Ed.

ED

Chuck us it, then.

(PHIL gets a CD, passes it to ED, who puts it on. It is loud and pulsey. They go off-road and drive to the picnic spot. They get out of the car, DOM and GEN unmerge and they settle down with salads, wine and food.)

(NOBODY is there, taking the piss out of the geese.)

MORAY

Who are you?

NOBODY

Nobody.

MORAY

Well fuck off, then.

NOBODY

Alright.

(NOBODY fucks off)

CHAPTER 8: WORK

The dialogue between the Saints
Sets sparks in office doors.
From boss who in his spare time paints
To those who Hoover floors.

Whispered fancies and the rest
Inspire a sandwich break.
Will I pass the safety test?
And is the new guy fake?

Tap and tap and enter key.
Swallowing my phlegm.
Am I the one who's really free
Or is it only them?

Mike decided, as Whistle had advised, to explore. He wandered away from the Mall towards the Coast and found some other buildings. The first one he saw was Duty. The front was modern and smart-looking, made of limestone with tinted windows. This part was called Commuting. The bit behind was a warehouse called The Ol'factory. Walking around the side, he went to The Ol'factory first.

Above the entrance to The Ol'factory was a sign that read SOCK OFFING. Inside were long lines of squashy benches in rows, with people sitting on them. Everyone was putting on and taking off socks. Sock after sock after sock. Sporty socks, spotty socks, black socks, white socks and woolly socks. He went over to an empty space and had a go. Some of the socks smelt nice, some of cheese and some of rice pudding. A bell went and everyone stopped and began leaving through different exits. He left too and went to Commuting instead.

The ground floor of Commuting was dedicated to paperwork and mirrors. He went in and was shown to a desk in a crowded room. He was told that his name was Mike and that he was to look into the mirror held up in front of him. He was surprised and pleased with his name and appearance and was told to go into a crowded court and try and find a perfect mate; he would know when he found them. Once he had found his mate, he was to report back to the desk to await further instructions, involving much paperwork and mirrors.

Above the crowd were six big machines into which a person could climb and view the people below. After he'd bustled around for a bit, he found himself in a short queue to the machines. Once at the front, a Guardian helped him into a machine. Each arm and leg was attached to splints with sensors, and there was a strap around his waist. He was raised up above the crowd and could see it clearly. When he moved, the machine greatly exaggerated each of his movements. Just a twitch of the leg and it shot forward. Soon he was in a full stride, legs and arms stretching boldly, though the machine stayed in the same spot. He was stunned by the thrill and power of it, all the while looking around for his perfect mate. Exhausted after half an hour, he was helped down by a Guardian and told to report back to the desk.

At the desk, he was told to go upstairs and have a meal, and try a different machine later. He had a tasty meal with a bunch of similarly dressed men and women (quite smart, like him) and got on very well with them.

After he said goodbyes he wondered off and saw what he assumed to be MLAR, because of its eight-sides, one left open.

Outside it was a group of weirdly dressed individuals, in oddly fitting clothes, hopping about and biting their nails. One at a time they went in, leaving before the next one went in. Mike watched. He heard raised voices but couldn't make out what was said. He caught a glimpse of the Guardian inside. His hair was grey and he wore spectacles. It was Mume Bibstripe but Mike would learn that later on.

Mike walked over to the eight sided building, and happened upon a Guardian to the side of it. He wore a uniform of sorts and had a protective jacket on, and some tools around his person. Eager to meet new sorts, he began a conversation with him. The nature of his task was rather grave, relating as it was, to dangerous persons. His eyes widened as he explained The Tank. The Tank was where someone would go if they had committed a Crime. For example, a Guardian would be extremely displeased if you, say, stabbed someone fiercely with a pencil. Crime, like this, was punishable by a spell in the Tank. The Tank was a large water tank in which one spent a sentence of time as punishment for committing Crime. The Tank was full of water and inmates stood at the bottom in weighted shoes until they had paid for their Crime. They were supplied with food and air (by pipes) but otherwise there was little to do. Inmates were able to see each other but the Tank had no fish and conversation is all there was to overweigh the boredom. Mike saw that he should obey his better instincts which, thank goodness, were fully intact.

Saying bye to the Guardian, he averted himself and noticed, near a tree, a young man climbing into what looked like a public litter bin. Curious to find out more, he went over to the bin and climbed in himself, seeing no potential harm in the expedition.

CHAPTER 9: SOB

I saw your heart – at once a goal
Inflated in my mind.
I found the girls outdated, cold.
They made me feel unkind.

Where were you, young boy?
My memory alive
With lunches, cavort and ahoy!
Alone I'll have to strive.

Just because you're absent now,
Knickers come to nought.
When we're one I am a cow.
Sacred, funny, taught.

Mike found himself passing through a layer of rubbish
then falling to the bottom of a large, black, wet cave.
He picked himself off the ground in front of a wooden
pulpit which was raised slightly, hid behind a column
of rock and viewed the scene. Behind the pulpit was an
enormous man with dark hair, wearing a black cloak.

"You have been a twerp and a berk, if I may say so?" boomed the man, the Devil, seemingly into the air. A lad was taking off his shoes and socks and dripping a clear liquid on to the top of his feet. He laughed out loud at the Devil then kind of blubbed.

"You find this amusing do you, you disgusting pervert?" bellowed the Devil. The lad gulped and swallowed, stuffing the little bottle into his jeans pocket. The Devil's assistant appeared: neat dark hair and a wobbly lower lip.

"Hang on…" said the assistant to the Devil.

"I'm not taking this," said the lad, starting to looking around. He found a spiral, stone staircase in the corner and began to climb it. Mike followed him up, but not before saying, "Hi. I'm Mike. I might see you later," and doing a little dance to the Devil and hurrying off.

"Are they going to give me a cow bell or not?" boomed the Devil to his assistant. The sound drifted up.

The lad and Mike emerged outside, by some trees near the bin. The lad had obviously himself and he'd also left his shoes and socks down there.

"I'm Lad," said Lad, and offered him his hand.

"Mike," he said, shaking it.

"Do you want to get some SOB? Mine's nearly run out."

He explained that SOB was an intoxicant that came in a little bottle with a pipette. You dropped a few drops of the liquid on to the tops of your bare feet and it did funny things to you. It could be sourced from a booth near the trees. All you had to do was go up to the man in the booth, pull a really stupid face, and he would give you a bottle of SOB. Mike was interested and decided to give it a go. He went to the booth, saw the man and produced a ludicrous, stupid face at him. The man smiled, bent down under the counter then handed him a bottle of SOB.

It wasn't long before he had his socks off and was dropping the clear liquid on to his feet. The first thing he did was laugh out loud. Then he began to go weak at the knees and began scanning around the place, looking for adventure. He looked apologetically at Lad then hastened towards the bin, scrambled into it and fell again to the bottom of the cave.

"I've been waiting for you," intoned the Devil. Mike's eyes were large and wet with expectation. Just then a phone rang and the assistant brought it over to the Devil, who answered it.

The Devil looked at Mike as he spoke. "It's your mother... No, he hasn't... No... Yes... Positive... Yes... No... Yes... No... Bye."

Mike laughed and simultaneously a set of plastic, clackety, toy false teeth fell to the ground between the Devil and his assistant.

"I've told Graham to fix them! How many times do I have to tell him?! We don't want the teeth any more! I mean, God! It's driving me mad!" shouted the Devil. Mike was feeling hilarious for a moment when he heard Lad shouting from above, "I've got your shoes!". He saw Lad's shoes and socks, too, and grabbed them.

"Pillock!" yelled the Devil as Mike dashed for the stairs.

Lad told Mike all about Slime House as they took more SOB together. He persuaded him that it was a great place to go: you could stay there as long as you liked. They walked off together, stumbling and laughing, eventually reaching a big square building from which much activity could be heard.

In the doorway was a man in swimming trunks standing beside a giant gong. He hit it each time someone in Slime House had a thoroughly good time. Lad and

Mike stayed in Slime House for four days. Exhausted, they emerged, too tired to say goodbye properly. Mike sat under a tree, waved Lad goodbye, then fell asleep.

CHAPTER 10: BELLS

The temperance of forgiveness comes
At such a lovely price.
If only we could say it once
And have the same chance twice.

I love the way you hold your head
And speak in gentle tone.
The way your conduct has been led
And why you're not alone.

Forgive me if I go astray,
It's not an easy vice.
The best love has a slow delay
And thanks for the advice.

Mike woke up under the tree, refreshed, and decided to continue his journey. After a short walk he noticed a beautiful building, the music of bells drifting from its roof. Beside it on a lawn was a crowd of assorted people chattering. Self consciously he walked through the crowd and into the building. It was beautiful and ornate inside, decorated with paintings and architectural features of grace and simplicity. The nave had wooden pews facing an altar at the far end. There was an air of lightness and calm. This was a place where he felt his desires were achievable.

He had a feeling that here was the very essence of Hero. It seemed all were welcome here, Guardian or not. Since his birthday party and finding himself in Hero, the hunger he had was manifest. Whistle had said that everything began in Eyes, the world of Ideas, and Mike's desires were for beauty, romance, laughter and the infinite. Eyes was infinite, but the hunger in Hero could be "unnameable, demonic, divine and human," as she had said. Perhaps it was the beauty of the building and the style of its interior that captivated Mike and the sight of so many faces and the sounds. How could he quench an infinite hunger? The only way he knew how, with beauty and the senses.

He sat down at the back and noticed a queue of people at the altar. At the front was a Guardian who had a few quiet words with each person, then dinged his cow bell. The Guardian was dressed in amazingly coloured robes. Mike noticed Whistle at the front of the queue and took a sharp intake of breath. The Guardian in robes said to her in clear English "Have compassion on your fellow beings," then hit his cow bell. Whistle was silent. A few moments later she left the church.

Other worshipers began to leave the church, people of all ages, shapes and colours, as music from an organ began to fill the air. Mike left, too, and bells could be heard chiming from the roof tower outside. The mood outside was celebratory. People were greeting each other, talking and smiling and some people were hugging each other. Farewells were made and Mike noticed Whistle walking off arm in arm with a bearded man. At the end of the green they stopped and he watched as they chatted.

Mike finally plucked up the courage to go over to Whistle and interrupted with a "Hi". She introduced Mike to a group of people. One of them was a young woman about his age. She wasn't a Guardian but took a keen interest in Mike. They talked about the bell's Guardian's beautiful robes. Mike and the young woman, whose name was Mary, arranged to meet in a couple of days in the Mall, as they got on so well.

A Conversation Between The Bearded Man, Paddy, and Whistle.

PADDY

Just stay there a moment will you?

WHISTLE

Why does Zero always fall short of the mark?

PADDY

He never does, darling.

WHISTLE

It's sponge isn't it?

PADDY

I haven't blinked for ages.

WHISTLE

Did you see that?

PADDY

Yes. Hey! Mike's just fallen in love.

WHISTLE

Oh my God. I've just thought of another word.

PADDY

What is it?

WHISTLE

Mellish.

PADDY

What does it mean?

WHISTLE

Let me see...It's what you've achieved the moment your eyes meet with a stranger you've just smiled at in a crowd when something you've both shared is so pleasing you can only smile and look at someone you've never seen before but you have to look at them and smile because it's so good but it's not so much an achievement but it's what someone's, that person's smile looks like when you look at them.

PADDY

That's good.

Paddy walked off into the countryside, shrinking into the distance.

CHAPTER 11: THE COAST

Misanthropic moves and curves
Deceive men every day.
It's best to be the one who loves
Than one who lets love stray.

Fighting comes to most, I know,
But loving comes to all.
You don't have to be a so and so
Or even be that tall.

Gardens are the best, my friend.
You'll find one in the town.
Flowers help the soul to mend.
The obverse of a frown.

Later on, Mike spotted two men walking towards where he believed the coast was. One of the men was tall, the other short. Both were wearing dark suits, dark ties and white shirts. The tall one had, protruding from the back of his jacket, a short metal rod with a wire noose dangling from it. Both men wore enormous wooden clogs. He walked behind them, close enough that he could hear some of their conversation, but far enough away not to draw attention to himself. They were talking about the different uses of slime. Slime House was mentioned, (with giggles and snorts of laughter) and spots and candles.

"Bringing up phlegm's on the increase."
"Where does it come from?"
"It's in the slime."
"How do they get it in there?"
"Can't tell you that," said the other.
"There's always a woman."
"Yes."
"There's always a woman somewhere."
"That's right."
"Somewhere, there's always a woman."
"Mmm," said the men.

They had arrived at the coastal area. Mike let the men walk on and noticed a small arcade where there were some machines with attractive flashing lights and colourful noises. He walked up to one and started pushing some of the buttons. It was called the Yummy Tummy Machine. Pleasant noises and four bright flashes. A card came out of the machine with four photos of Mike on it, looking rather handsome. Just then an arm with a boxing glove came shooting out of the front, hitting him in the stomach. He vomited and felt rather spaced out. The men looked on.

"You get that?"

"Yeah."

"It must be a myth."

"Twat," came the voices of the Men in Dark Suits.

Mike saw a pogo stick on the ground, grabbed it and pogoed his way on further. Overhead, the meteor flew. A large, flaming ball of rock, decreasing in size as it went. Descending over the people that were around, everyone went "Wooaahh!" as it flew. A couple of moments later and, now no bigger than a match box, it landed with a rattle in a gigantic plastic bowl which was positioned on the coast, right near the water's edge. There was a round of applause from the people. He was walking towards the coast and could just make out a Guardian walking up to the base of the gigantic plastic bowl, which must have been three storeys high. The Guardian took a U-shaped magnet from inside his jacket and placed it underneath the bowl, right in the centre. As the magnet touched the bottom of the bowl, the tiny meteor rock exploded into ten thousand litres of slime, filling the bowl. The audience was awed.

Next, he visited three different wooden huts, which were around that part of the coastal area.

HUT 1: Messrs Masseurs.
Mike went in and had a lovely massage.

HUT 2: God's Hut.
He went up to this hut and peered through the window. Inside was a fat, bald man sitting on cushions, surrounded by dozens of gold and silver cow bells. There was a sign above the door that said "GOD". A man and a woman burst out of the door clutching cameras, turning around as they fled.
"Get that camera outta here!," boomed God.
Mike looked in and entered. God looked magnificent in his robes.
"Hi. I'm God," He said. "But you can call me Graham. This is the pre-life. There is no afterlife. Just a pre-life. It's the best we could do."
God explained to Mike that he was a supreme being and that he was head of all the Guardians. This was probably due to his extreme personal charisma and

longevity. He neither quite fitted into The School of Manners nor The School of the Fool.

When someone had proved themselves, they could either stay on and be a Guardian or leave Hero and start a real life which would include suffering. Each Guardian had a cowbell and could ding it when they had seen that someone was complete enough to move on when they were a full egg, as God put it. The cowbells in there weren't really his and he couldn't give them out. He just kept them in there to make himself feel important. However, Mike learnt much from God and felt like he needed the loo so went to:

HUT 3: Ull.

This was a wooden hut with a veranda, completely painted white. From within could be heard soft piano music. He went in and had a poo. There was paper and everything. He felt good.

After leaving Ull, he wondered a little and saw a white and grey port cabin from which he heard smashing noises and male voices. He walked up the few steps to its door onto which was pinned a piece of paper with "Rue Room" scrawled on it. He knocked, paused and entered. Inside were two young men in shirts and boxer shorts throwing large hard-boiled eggs at each other, as hard as they could. Wham! "That fucking hurt," said one. Both had bruises and eggs were everywhere. They seemed to enjoy it, with grins. Mike said "Sorry" and bowed out of the room.

CHAPTER 12: THE GIRLS

Causes do to mental clout
What music does to love.
Banishes instinctual doubt
And pleases one above.

You cannot choose your duty, though,
It will come to you.
Duty comes from where we grow,
We wish they only knew.

In the end it doesn't end,
Everything's the same.
We're only trying to make things mend.
Children see the gain.

Some of the female Guardians went for a drink, in a club near the Coast.

The Girls:

Miss. Me   Quiet
Miss. Demeanour   Loud

Miss. Chief	Sad
Miss. Guided	Friendly
Miss. Understood	Charming and loopy
Miss. Stress	Sassy and smart
Miss. Nomer	Intelligent and wise
Miss. Adventure	Firey
Miss. Judge	Officious and strong

There are other female Guardians but these are the ones who like to go out together.

Mike wandered over to the seating area near where the Girls were and noticed that he was turning invisible. As his clothes weren't, he took advantage of the situation and stripped off, before having a thoroughly enjoyable time singing karaoke.

While Mike was still invisible, he listened to the following conversation:

CHIEF
Alright?
GUIDED
You can't imagine how mad it is not having talked to the Flourishes.

CHIEF

Catch hasn't said anything to you has she?

GUIDED

All she said was that if Stressy hadn't arched her way into the garden then none of this would have happened.

CHIEF

Don't hamper for God's sake. Stressy doesn't even know when she's around and when she's not.

GUIDED

The Flourishes don't seem to mean anything to her.

CHIEF

Will you stop worrying about it?

GUIDED

You know what's going to happen? Catch will stare at her so long she'll beam back so hard she won't even realise she's had it. I reckon all the pollen flasks she has will spark so hard into the light she'll have to wear a golden mask till it hits her face.

CHIEF

You're probably right, dear.

STRESS

Who's going to have the beer?

GUIDED

The Golden Cup.

NOMER

The Mask of Fate.

UNDERSTOOD

The Electrical Hat you can stand in.

ADVENTURE

The Mighty Glue.

CHIEF

The Hungry Slapper.

DEMEANOUR

The Waving Sailor.

(UNDER takes out her cowbell, dinks it, and they start drinking)

UNDER

When are the spoons arriving? You know, the ones that are supposed to be being delivered to the hall for the Ball.

GUIDED

What spoons?

UNDERSTOOD

They're coming at about six thirty I think.

DEMEANOUR

Really?

UNDERSTOOD

Stressy, you know don't you?

DEMEANOUR

Three hundred and sixty.

NOMER
All of them.
UNDERSTOOD
Yeah.
GUIDED
Um. About six thirty.
UNDERSTOOD
I was just wondering how we're going to get through three hundred and sixty spoons.
GUIDED
It'll be fine.
UNDERSTOOD
Have you seen them?
GUIDED
It won't matter. You'll see them.
STRESS
You'll have to see them.
(They pause to drink their beers.)
UNDERSTOOD
So. Let's see. We've got all those cheesecakes for the ball. 60 strawberry. 40 cherry. 80 gooseberry and 20 raspberry. 30 plum. 50 blackberry. 30 blackcurrant and 30 apple. 80 blue berry and 40 sloe.
CHIEF
And the tomatoes.

UNDERSTOOD

There are 40 tomato flans that need the pastries and all the stuff to go with the tomatoes, and the potatoes are being flown in tomorrow. There's some confusion about whether there's enough room for the plane to land.

NOMER

Cleopatra's noice.

(UNDERSTOOD explodes beer from her mouth with a lurch forward.)

DEMEANOUR

Thanks for that.

GUIDED

Have you seen Miss. Calculation. I saw her at the echelons by the Mall. She was there yesterday above the School of How to Fall in Love.

ME

She's beautiful. It's like she's from a dream. Like one I had the other day. There was this woman. She was walking along and her hair was kind of…marching. She was walking too but her hair was sort of doing it independently on top of her head, like it was marching. At the same pace. With her.

GUIDED

She's beautiful.

CHIEF
I don't think she's beautiful.
GUIDED
She doesn't smoke.
CHIEF
Who does smoke?
ADVENTURE
I smoke.
DEMEANOUR
You're the only one.
ADVENTURE
I will give up.

Mike began to become visible again so quickly dressed, wondering what a cigarette could be, then headed back along the main avenue to the School of Manners.

CHAPTER 13: THE CONVERSATION

The poltergeist of freedom falling
Wastes a lot of time.
What's the point without a calling?
Cycling without rhyme.

Freeway, byway, highway, gate.
Freezing food and cows.
There's fire in the morning grate
And lots of time to browse.

Eventually I'm tired at last
And waiting for my pit.
Digesting food and making fast,
The candle still is lit.

In The School of Manners Mike listened to a radio
program. It was an interview with the Guru Mume
Bibstripe. We join it half way through.

SPUD
So, Mume. How's the miming going?

MUME

We're doing a piece about old age at the moment; by the coast. The test audience are window cleaners and physiotherapists.

SPUD

And I gather you're playing the lead.

MUME

That's right.

SPUD

So, Mume. What is it exactly you do?

MUME

Well, I'm a kind of guru.

SPUD

Really. Are you the sort of person who thinks the whole of Britain should be landscaped?

MUME

No.

SPUD

That's good.

MUME

Thanks.

SPUD

So. What are your beliefs?

MUME

Well. I have principles. Principal among them being is to have "Gosh".

SPUD

Right.

MUME

And rug hurtling. I hurtle rugs.

SPUD

Gosh...

MUME

Ha ha. And tea towels.

SPUD

You hurtle tea towels.

MUME

No, I just like them.

SPUD

And is there rug hurtling in the show?

MUME

Yes.

SPUD

Is it difficult to perform rug hurtling in a small space?

MUME

It's not too difficult. We just hurtle the rugs into a wall.

SPUD

I see. How many people are there in the show?

MUME

Well, we have audience participation.

SPUD

Are they good?

MUME

They're very good. Not perfect. But polite; which is as near to perfect as you can be. Yummy, essentially. (Mume farts)

SPUD

You pass wind like it's going out of fashion!

MUME

Thank you.

SPUD

Tea?

MUME

Thanks.

SPUD

I gather one of your mimes, Mume, is of a cow.

MUME

That's right.

SPUD

Doing what exactly?

MUME

Climbing down a ladder.

SPUD

Don't be ridiculous.

MUME

No, it's true.

SPUD

Christ, it's a world out there.

MUME

You're right.

SPUD

So you're essentially playing yourself.

MUME

Yes.

SPUD

So. You say you're a guru; what exactly do you know?

MUME

Well. I know that the belly button is the most perfect proof that the division of man isn't necessarily asymmetrical.

SPUD

Scary. Are you a Guardian?

MUME

Yes.

SPUD

What does Andy think?

MUME

He's very supportive.

SPUD

So he should be.

MUME

Will you come and see the show.

SPUD

I will definitely go and see it. Oh, by the way. Have you got any prophesies?

MUME

Yup. In the future, gelatine will inspire a billion children to make music.

SPUD

Wow. You got any understatements?

MUME

I've got a few.

SPUD

Ha ha ha.

MUME

You forgot to make the tea.

SPUD

So I did.

Mike switched off the radio and talked to a few people there, then headed to the Mall again to meet Mary.

CHAPTER 14: ESTABLISHMENTS

Establishments are here to stay,
They make us feel alright.
From tennis, boozers, Lords or Hay,
They're run by people bright.

Reject them at your peril, geeze,
They'll always serve the state,
Put the cultural lot at ease
And please the good and great.

If you think you're better than
The groups who make the cheese
Then form your own and tell your gran,
Your best friend and Louise.

Along the centre of the nave of the Mall was a long strip of grass. I shall list the things Mike did in the Mall, before meeting up with Mary, starting with what he saw on the grass:

STATIONERY. People were gathered on the lawn with stationery in their hands and littered around the grass was more stationery. The activity seemed to consist of throwing the items as high into the air as possible and either catching them or letting them land on the ground. The men and women wore shirts and suits and delighted in the way the stationery landed. Pens, staplers, blocks of paper. What struck Mike was the height to which the computer was thrown and the attractive way it stuck into the ground when it landed, with a pleasing sound.

CIGARETTES. A small shop lined with thousands of individual cigarettes and a sign saying "Cigarettes for non-smokers. Once you try one you'll never want to smoke another one ever again." He did try one and it made him cough and choke. The advert was right.

ART GALLERY. This gallery had the word METAL as its logo, in sharp letters. It was a gallery of smells, despite the attractive black and white pictures on the walls. He went in, was handed a pair of dark goggles and was surrounded by other young adults, similarly goggled, walking around and bumping into one another, sniffing all over the place, getting a whiff of the art-smells on offer. He felt very cool.

THE SCHOOL OF HOW TO FALL IN LOVE. This was a very small cinema in which was repeated three very short films, each about the courting rituals of a man and a woman.

FILM 1: Set in a hotel bedroom, a woman walks into the room. The footage has been filmed and played in reverse, so the walking looks peculiar. She sits at a dressing table and begins to make up her face. On the right is a man sitting on a bed. He watches her coolly. As she puts on one last touch to her lips, she swivels round to the man. Two chairs and a table are sucked into his penis. They stare at one another.

FILM 2: A man and a woman face each other in a small room. Behind each of them is a heavy green curtain. The woman coyly looks away towards her curtain, in which time the man whips out a bunch of flowers. The woman admires them and looks coyly away again. Next time the man produces a bigger bunch of flowers. This happens several times, the woman's curtain rising at the bottom in a flirty way each time.

FILM 3: A man with a cup and saucer approaches a woman. He kisses the woman on the mouth. He drops the cup and saucer.

He watched each film three times before moving to:

PARADOX. The shop sign read "Every Paradox Has A Dark Side". He walked in and fell ten feet into a large dark room in complete weightlessness. There were red, orange and green orbs of light floating round. Hovering inside was a man in a safari jacket and trousers. They began to talk about the weather and such things. He was charming. Then he helped Mike up to the doorway and let him out. Charming.

THE SCHOOL OF OBLIVION AND ROUNDED EDGES was a shower of squashy balls, cubes and pyramids of different colours.

SEX CRITICS. Go there and be analysed or analyse. Also general appearance criticism.

CHILDREN AND TV. Mike went in and minded two children who were watching television: a stream of adverts for bodily functions.
"Want to clear your throat? Try coughing." And others. Mike felt completely comfortable and at ease here, total security, it was only he had arranged to meet Mary so he went to:

HICCUPS AND SOUP LIMITED. Mike and Mary met up and had a meal. The bread and butter was especially good. They spoke in normal English.

Having had enough of the Mall, they went to the Theatre to see " The World's Shortest Play."
The theatre is full. Hush. The curtain goes up. A drawing room. Lamps. Armchairs. We can tell it's raining outside. Two gentlemen are seated.
First gentleman: "Writing a play is making who you least like likeable."
Second gentleman: "Is it?"
The End.

CHAPTER 15: THE HISTORY HOUSE

The poet sees his every word
Described upon the page,
And whether he be right or not
He versifies the age.

His wisdom may be suspect,
His wits may show him small,
But treat him with a kind respect
And he will tell it all.

From flowers by the trenches dug
To romance in the dunes,
And tragedy told by the hearth
All set in worldly tunes.

Finding their way back past the Mall, Mike and Mary
went up to the huge façade of Manners, Silly and Fool,
and decided to take a walk round the back.

There was a big nothingy area of mud and gravel which
they crossed, walking further in to night. Beyond that

were lawns divided by a gravel path which led to a very small castle called The History House.

Along the path was a large zig-zagging crack leading up to the house.

The first thing Mike and Mary saw was a largish rabbit hopping forwards towards the building. It hopped over and around the crack in the ground, moving left and right.

"I'm not gonna follow a bloody rabbit," said Mike. The rabbit hopped along.

Mike wondered if the crack actually reached the house and if the whole building itself might actually crack in two.

"What the fuck's that?" he said, looking down at the crevice in the ground.

"Don't worry, Hun. It's not your fault," said Mary. Mike exploded a little "Ha, ha," and Mary said "What's that?."

"Sorry, no. It's nothing," he said, clearing his throat.

They moved towards The History House. There was a large moon behind the turrets of the house. Two bats flapped unnecessarily in front of it and silhouetted. On the left of the building was a car; to the right was a group of termite mounds on a lawn. Further to the right, under a lean to, two horses stood, tethered.

They entered the castle door.

"Hi! Come in! I'm Henry," came a voice. Up walked an ant-eater; his snout was rather awkward but he had good teeth.

"I feel odd," said Mike.

"Perhaps you'd feel better in these?" said Henry, and led them to a side room.

"Here. Put these on."

In a minute, Mike and Mary were wearing puffy orange pantaloons.

"Do we have to wear these?" said Mike.

"It looks like it," said Mary.

"Perhaps you'd like a tour?" said Henry. A woman walked into the hall from a side door with four dogs on leads.

"This is Stella," said Henry.

"I'm just taking this lot out," she said.

Mike peered into the side room and saw kennels, dog stuff and hooks on the walls. Stella was wearing country clothes; her age about forty.

Down to the left, Henry led Mike and Mary along a corridor. Mike heard clackety noises, laughter and chatting. Henry opened a door (it was a larder) and they all saw three skeletons dancing around, laughing and gossiping.

"Will you stop pissing about!" shouted Henry. The skeletons stared back at him.

Mike noticed that around the whole house were neat mouse holes in the skirting boards but neither Mike nor Mary saw any mice. All the rooms had spiders' webs and spiders around the beams and in the corners, but that was by the by.

At the back of the History House on the ground floor was a tall square room with an enormous wood-burning stove in it. It kept the whole house warm. Next to it, sitting around a small table, were three monks in robes, drinking tea.

Henry led Mike and Mary upstairs to a spacious dining room with kitchen. Henry put a record on the decks to the side and music filled the room.

"I've no idea what's going on," said Mike.
"Whisky?" said Henry.
"No, thanks," said Mike.
"No, thanks," said Mary.
"How long has History House been here?" said Mike.
"Well," said Henry, "It's almost as old as the hills. No. Actually it's about two hundred years old. What would you really like to talk about?"

"Well. Lots of things, actually. Mostly about purpose. I need to have a purpose. What's my responsibility?"

"Responsibility?" said Henry. "Who to?"

"To myself. Family. Guardians. Hero. Whatever's out there."

"Why do you want to be responsible?" said Henry.

"Well. Umm. Because I don't want to be a waste of space. And I've got this body. My body is part of the Natural world. I'm part of the world. I want to fit in."

"Why did you mention your body?" said Henry.

"Well. It's sort of why I'm here. I need food and shelter and all that stuff but there is always desire. We need to sort that out. We need to sort it out but I do believe desire isn't the most important thing. It must just be part of life. There must be a connection between desire and purpose in the world. We can't just be desirous. We must justify our places in the world with responsibility, purpose and meaning," said Mike.

"So you think having purpose, responsibility and meaning is the same as fitting in?" said Henry.

"Yes," said Mike.

"Golly," said Henry.

"I know," said Mike.

"You can start by doing the washing up. The windows need cleaning and the floor needs a mop, too," said Henry.

Mike started. Mary read a book. Half an hour later and it was done.

"I'm tired," said Mike.
"Take a bath," said Henry.
"I want one, too," said Mary.

Mike and Mary took baths, one following the other. They also cut their nails, combed their hair and brushed their teeth.

Next to the bathroom door was a light switch on the wall for the attic, which you could get to with the step-ladder leaning against the wall and led up to the square door in the ceiling. They moved back to the dining room.

Mike looked out of the window to the back of History House. He saw, lit by the moon, a swimming pool next to another lawn. The pool was half covered by black, floating leaves.

Beyond the pool was a fenced paddock; beyond that were dark woods from where came the sound of night birds and beyond the woods were dark hills. Mike was lost in reverie.

At the table again, Henry elsewhere, Mike and Mary played Angels for a while. They found separate bedrooms, each making their bed before getting in and going to sleep. Sweet dreams.

CHAPTER 16: THEY MEET

Expression puts life on a tilt,
Closer to the heart
Of purpose and the essence
Of playing our own part.

Sentimental is the best,
Deserved, required, attained.
No kitsch and it's hard to rest,
Just look at the ordained.

But express these things we shall,
Better out than in.
Careful now, the tribe is small
And children make a din.

The next day Mike and Mary met on the gravel in front
of Silly. The sun was high. Other people were around
but they were apart enough not to be overheard.

MIKE
I love you.

MARY

I know.

MIKE

Did you enjoy History House?

MARY

Yeah.

MIKE

Right.

MARY

I love you, too.

MIKE

What shall we do?

MARY

Together?

MIKE

Yeah.

MARY

Anything.

MIKE

What do you want to do?

MARY

Be together.

MIKE

That's what I want.

MARY

Me too.

MIKE

We haven't known each other that long.

MARY

I want to know you more than ever.

MIKE

And me you.

MARY

Do you think we can get to know each other?

MIKE

Yes. That's what we both want.

MARY

Yes.

MIKE

What about the future?

MARY

Who knows?

MIKE

I am frightened.

MARY

Me too.

MIKE

I'll have to find work.

MARY

Me too.

MIKE

I love you.

MARY

I love you too.

MIKE

We can see each other tomorrow.

MARY

Yes.

MIKE

OK.

(They kiss)

MARY

Bye.

MIKE

Bye.

They each needed some space for a bit.

CHAPTER 17: BRAVERY

The unaccustomed soldier says
His heart is not yet hard.
He doesn't know the answer's "Yes",
And that it's in the yard.

It takes such time to get it right.
Such pains are hard to take.
He breaks his balls to get to fight.
It doesn't make him fake.

Eventually he makes his mark,
Distinction and the grade.
We love his knowledge of the dark,
Transcended, fought and made.

Later on, Mike was alone in Hero and began to feel a
new sensation that he couldn't quite identify. It was
from within and he began to think about MLAR. What
if this feeling grew? Like a cramp or sour taste he tried
to pass it off as nothing but realised that he couldn't
ignore it. It felt like a flaw in his character and wondered if there could be a trace of evil in this growing

feeling of madness. Was he going mad? Indeed, was he becoming evil?

His walking speeded up, now along one of the main avenues of Hero. In the distance he saw MLAR and was relieved to see no queue outside it. Very vaguely he saw the figure of Mume Bibstripe in the chair and a shaft of light reflected off Mume's spectacles into Mike's eyes.

"Slow down," he thought.

"There is no suffering in Hero," he remembered Whistle saying.

"This hunger can be infinite, unnameable, demonic, divine, human…"

"Until you satisfy yourself you will not suffer."

All these words of Whistle came back to him.

What was it that Tony had said? "If you feel the need to talk to someone, if you feel the need to escape, to say whatever you want…"

In Hero there could be no room for this feeling Mike was experiencing. It grew in him like a flame. He thought of God. He thought of Mary. No consolation. He got to MLAR.

He felt so excited. This couldn't really be happening. An overwhelming tension flooded Mike's mind as he approached Mume in his chair. As if his brain might explode at the sheer exhilaration of this feeling.

MUME
So tell me...
MIKE
Mike.
MUME
What exactly did you want to say?
MIKE
Well. It's sort of...well...

Mike, then finding his voice, his eyes almost wobbling in their sockets, glared at Mume and expelled from his being a terrific, eager, howling and loudly piercing scream.

"EEEEEEEEEEAAAAARRRRGGGHHH-
HHH!!!!"

Next, a pause. He had some memories. These were they.

Himself as a little boy in a tiny toilet trying to go for a poo.

Children in a bedroom with bunks playing with toys on the floor.

An empty single bedroom.

Lots of people watching a tiny telly.

A steaming hot kitchen with flame wok cooking and a man and a woman.

Himself lying on a bed.

The next thing Mike found himself at the bottom of a deep river, the Nile. The water was dark and silty. There was pressure. He looked left and saw a fish lurk then selfishly dart away. He looked right and saw the head of God on the river bed. It looked straight at Mike, grinned, then looked away.

Mike began to rise to the surface of the water. It got lighter, the pressure lightened, he moved upwards through the water.

He saw a boat on the water in the mid-distance.

AWAKE.

He looked at Mume, sitting there in his spectacles on the chair in front of him.

MUME
Tea?
MIKE
Yes, please.
MUME
There's nothing funny about a cup of tea.
MIKE
No.
MUME
Now. How do you feel?
MIKE
Better.
MUME
Is there anything you'd like to ask?
MIKE
Can you tell me about sex?
MUME
You start apart.
MIKE
Don't you?!

MUME

I suppose.

MIKE

Yes.

MUME

Respectfully.

MIKE

Apparently.

MUME

And can you imagine it in a garden?

MIKE

Imagine if you blinked at the same time.

MUME

All four eyes.

MIKE

The caution of movement is really a passion.

MUME

Not being weak is the singular defence against duality.

MIKE

Yes. Is skill an atrocity?

MUME

Yes. I think so.

MIKE

But marital arts can't do without a singular spirit of mind, or there's a shallow duality.

MUME
And that won't do.
MIKE
No.
MUME
Finally the resolution of home magic defeats ends.
MIKE
And we brush up a bit
MUME
That's it.

Mume dinked his little bell.

Over.
Beginning.

CHAPTER 18: OUTDOORS

Sustainable ecology
Has something in it, no?
Depend on pharmacology
And let the damn things grow.

Fish and forests seem to me
To be the crux and pain.
Nourish them and you will see
That there is much to gain.

From lions we can learn a lot
And insects rule the world.
Think about your garden plot
And times it trillion fold.

The next day, Mike and Mary found a place in the countryside, away from the buildings, where there was a kind of outdoor festival of entertainments, games and refreshments. They saw five events, which were also displayed on a giant video screen:

FURNITURE FIGHTING

There was the feel of a village carnival. Standing around a grassy area, many with beers, was a group of people ready to watch Fighting With Furniture. First up was a young man versus a kitchen table. He came away better off than the table but had bruised and bloody knuckles. He was applauded and the broken table was taken away. Next up was the big fight. The biggest man versus the biggest table. The man wore a top hat and a fine suit and had a moustache. The table was mahogany, six legs and very stable. The man downed two pints before setting about the table with kicks and punches; it was terrifying to behold. It was a really tough fight: at least four minutes. By the end the table was shattered and the man was down on the ground. Applause.

Later there was a fight between a boy and a wooden chair. Eye patch; chair broken leg.

TABLE LAYING FESTIVAL

A round robin competition primarily for women and children. The different games included Gang Gasping, Bap Stacking and Flap Gapping. Win the Golden Fork. Compulsory cheating for the children.

SHREDDING

An arc of shredders was positioned on some grass with a man behind each one. The game involved taking off layers of clothing and shredding them. It was against the rules to disrobe at the same time as anyone else. The winner was the first naked man. A dog urinated nearby.

PEEVE FACTOR

To express "I am capable of being considerably more peeved than you." Men sat on chairs in a circle and were told to chat. When one of them felt anger at all, he was to stand up and spin, scratching his head. The women enjoyed it when two or more men did it at the same time.

HEN SPRINT

Performed at the end of the day, a group of eleven chickens race. Much support and cheering. 400 yards.

"How come it's not meters?"

"It goes back a long way."

Mary and Mike chat.

MARY

Thanks for coming to the outdoors with me.

MIKE
That's OK.
MARY
It was good.
MIKE
Did you like the games and everything?
MARY
Yeah.
MIKE
That guy really gave the table some!
MARY
Yeah!
MIKE
I thought the table was going to win!
MARY
That poor boy and the chair!
MIKE
He got poked in the eye.
MARY
Do you think he'll be alright?
MIKE
I'm sure he's fine.
MARY
And the hens!

MIKE

They can run really fast!

MARY

They're so sweet!

MIKE

Do you remember the Peeve Factor?

MARY

It was so funny watching those men getting up and scratching their heads.

MIKE

Yeah.

MARY

That's why they're so bald!

MIKE

Hang on!

MARY

What?

MIKE

I'm receding a bit too!

MARY

You're fine.

MIKE

Thanks.

(Pause)

MARY
I thought it was great.

(Mary gets out a book)

MARY
I'm reading this book by Mume Bibstripe.
MIKE
"I sold my soul to a salad but it works."
MARY
That's the one. The book's called *Feta Mystics*.
(He takes the book and reads aloud)
MIKE
"In my opinion the pen is mightier than the sword.
The camera is mightier than the pen. I don't know
what's mightier than the camera but it's pretty fuck-
ing mighty."

"There's always a woman. Somewhere, there's always
a woman. There's always a woman somewhere."

"If in doubt, and I'm sure you will be one day, keep
your memories. You can do what you like with the
rest."

"Culture is systemized passion."

(He breaks from reading)
Good book, Mary.
MARY
Yeah. He's canny isn't he, my old man?!

CHAPTER 19: THE BALL

The timeless essence of a man
Is born in early on.
Depending on the family plan
And how they get along.

Trouble mixes up the set.
Experience the pain.
One thing that you may regret
Will never come again.

Always there and older, too.
Body sees the day.
When it's time just say, "I do".
You'll never look away.

Mike and Mary went to the Guardian's Ball together, dressed in fine clothes. Meeting so many Guardians all in one place was a thrill. Flans were eaten in plenty and after eating was dancing.
Moray was one of the Guardians there.
"The thing is, there's no beauty without suffering. So you have to ask yourself, is there any beauty in Hero?"

Phil replied, "Sneezes can be fatal, so you have to make the most of your time and find beauty where ever you can. All Hero is beautiful. Until you become a Guardian, that is, which, to be honest, can be a real pain." He added that "Although we are all born in Eyes, we never really leave Eyes. Equally, even though we move on from Hero, our bodies never really leave it. We acquire suffering as an extra after we leave Hero, we acquire another layer of meaning, giving reality a truth. Your time after Hero is a reflection of your time there, even if you die young. Your age in Hero, even though it never changes, shows your future character."

The highlight of the evening was towards the end. There were some speeches but afterwards, when everyone was congregated, each Guardian took his or her teaspoon and threw it high into the air. Due to some magic, each teaspoon was propelled at just the right speed so that it stopped when it reached the ceiling and stuck there. Each teaspoon was at a slightly different angle, touching the high ceiling. A drum roll, a crash and the lights were dimmed. Five seconds later and a powerful light was shone on to the spoons. Each individual teaspoon reflected the light into a single beam.

360 individual teaspoons all casting beams of light in different directions, filling the hall with lines of light, crossing each other in a crazy pattern of silver light in the darkness; beams of light hitting the walls and the floor, lines everywhere. Massive applause and cheers and more music.

Reason got drunk and shouted "ALCHEMY!" as loudly as he could at everyone he met. Fucking Boring kept trying to meet new people by introducing himself and saying that Reliable was his middle name, which it was. The Busses were there. They were a couple who were architects and had quite a few friends. Ed and Mike had a chat:

MIKE
What star sign are you?
ED
I was born in the year of the lung.
MIKE
I'm an Aquarius.
ED
Do you like fish?
MIKE
Yes, I love 'em.

ED

Do you play a musical instrument?

MIKE

I play the chin.

A bow was thrown to him. He stroked it across his chin. It made different notes reflecting his thoughts. Ed was amused and delighted.

One of the chaps saw an old face. "Hello Constipation!"

"Make yourself presumable," said by two people independently of each other, loudly and at exactly the same time. The hubbub stopped and people stared.

Mike danced with Mary. This was amusing when some unpredictable music came on and they had wildly to improvise to each other's movements.

Mary has a chat with her friend Sarah.

MARY

I've met someone.

SARAH

Great. Is he interesting?

MARY

Clinically interesting.

SARAH

Is he clinically interested?

MARY

Yes, I think so.

SARAH

When did you meet him?

MARY

I think I've known him all my life.

SARAH

I saw him tonight.

MARY

He's a spoff.

SARAH

What's a spoff?

MARY

Like a spiff, but not as quite.

SARAH

Much better in my opinion.

MARY

Yes.

SARAH

But not as good.

MARY

Quite.

SARAH

So, he's not a spiv.

MARY

No.

SARAH

Good.

MARY

Yeah. I said let there be crisps and there wasn't. Then he just turned up!

SARAH

Did you dance?

MARY

We did a bit. Then someone put on Beethoven's 'Moonlight Sonata'. You can't dance to that. If you do you end up behaving utterly normally which is what I call Full Circle.

SARAH

Do you love him?

MARY

I love him too much.

SARAH

I suggest you have an orgasm with your head in a bucket of cold water.

MARY

He's as calm as a sausage. I'm as lusty as an apple. You seem as sceptical as a horse.

SARAH

Is he funny?

MARY

He's funnier than me put together.

SARAH

Sounds the perfect match.

MARY

I want to throw him in the air. Quite high.

SARAH

Have you had any arguments?

MARY

Something about poo, needles and a double edged camel. I don't want to go into it

SARAH

Right.

MARY

It's myself that keeps running away from myself.

SARAH

That's so awful.

MARY

He's a Fool.

SARAH

That's great. If a Fool could be an athlete too he wouldn't half be a genius.

MARY

You know exactly where you are with him.

SARAH

How's that?

MARY

Because he has absolutely no idea where he is.

SARAH

Really?

MARY

He clinically favours the foot which happens to be the wrong one. How can you be cynical about peppermint?

SARAH

Oh my God.

MARY

He suffers for his art but like all things takes it to extremes. Which leads me to believe there's nothing in his head except fluffy dildo trees.

SARAH

Does he know what beauty is?

MARY

He knows what it looks like.

SARAH

That's where you come in.

MARY

Ha ha ha.

SARAH

Anyway, that's great.

MARY

Thanks.

(They hug)

CHAPTER 20: LOVE

When love becomes pain
And trust becomes freedom
Make death your friend
And beauty your kingdom.

Of love enter slowly
Completely and fully.
Penetrate secrets
That lust will reveal.

When eyes become windows
And dreamscape is real
Have faith in the pain
That makes faithless insane.

After the ball: "Mary and I will be in Silly," said Mike. Near him, on the grass, was a pair of rollerblades. He put them on and headed towards the other end of Hero. First, he went to God's hut to see if he could advise anything. He wasn't in. On the way, he passed The School of Oblivion and Rounded Edges, the Scallum and the Arsy, Ull, the Mall, the Theatre, and saw ahead the large squares of The School of Manners and The School of The Fool. Silly was between them and as he approached, he heard pop music and saw a light show in the sky. There was a band playing on the roof of Silly, and as he got nearer he could hear it more clearly. There was a lead singer at the front, on the left was a man in a sort of white dressing gown doing a dance that resembled the ritual of making a cup of tea, a drummer at the back, other musicians and backing vocalists on the right.

In Silly's doorway he saw Mary. Fast, he got there and they hugged. An unknowable presence of time elapsed in blissful suspension.

CHAPTER 21: THE MORNING
AFTER THE NIGHT BEFORE

The lapidary hearth rug
Spins my funky head.
I'll be a horny love bug,
It makes me feel so dead.

Orgy go away my dear,
You and me or nought.
It's time we got all rudely queer
And naked slapstick fought.

The rest is downright timeless.
Out with it and so
We see the fact and loving bless
The aftermath and glow.

He wakes up. He's half dead. Still drunk with exhaustion, his eyes are fixed on the bulb of the bedside light. Mary gets up and walks to the other side of the room. He sees her, his eyes fixed on her head. But the bulb of the bedside light has stayed on his retina and he sees an orange blob where her head is. She leaves the room.

He walks to the top of the stairs, eyes puffy and mildly astonished. He says the word "Deck" and pauses. There is a small crescent of chocolate milkshake on his cheek.

He says, "I've just woken up down there."

From nowhere comes the voice of Mary.

"The world of the purple catastrophe."

"You're teasing," says Mike.

"Are you sure?"

"Yes, I am," says Mike.

"What does 'obv' mean?" says Mary.

"Thanks," he says.

"That's alright," she says.

"Fibres. Delicate. Monkey. The Mall," he says.

"In Jamaica the sand is so fine they use it as a deodorant."

"It's not what you are…" he says.

He hears a noise. He laughs.

Free from desire.

Downstairs, flicking through the local newspaper looking for something, he stops on this; looks at it, circles it, turns it upside down and looks at it again:

SOMETHING TO KILL
Rug Hurtling

Distance an avantash
Flat spin desired
MUST HAVE GOSH

He puts the newspaper down and sees in the next door room, Mary watching telly.

He pauses for a moment and is lost in time.

He looks down, pauses, picks up a knife from the table and in one movement throws it into the dart board. It sticks in.
The kitchen is a mess. The blind by the window has string dangling down on to the work surface. He tries to put the brown string back on to the top of the blind but has to reach forwards on tip toes and finds it difficult. "Bugger," he says. He fumbles with the string and eventually it stays put.

We find that he is standing on a huge flat screen telly which has been left on the floor. He looks down and sees clouds and sky on the screen. He steps off.

Mary enters the room.

They embrace.

CHAPTER 22: SOME YEARS LATER

Help me in my afterlife,
Help me in my death,
Help me in my day-to-day
And give me love and breath.

I love you for gentleness
And kindness in the light,
For loving in the evening
And tenderness of night.

Be my one and only
And give me peace of mind.
You are so very lovely
And generous and kind.

Some years later Mike and Mary are a couple, settled down and doing couple things like shopping, going to the theatre and drinking gins.

Mike asks Mary about her new car.
"Why's your car pink?"
"Why are your teeth brown?" replies Mary.

Over by the market and a small argument occurs.

"We've got too many limes!" says Mary.

"How can you have too many limes?!" screeches Mike.

They pop into a little art gallery as they're in town. A show of black and white prints with logos.

"Look at this one," says Mary, "it has a wonderful sense of contrast."

"No," says Mike, perturbed and wanting to get home immediately, something in the print obviously getting to him.

There is a certain amount of distaste in reality. Mike has a job. Beer, adults, cars, shirts, grit, nobs.

Later that evening and they go to the theatre. It's foreign. The stage: a nicely lit drawing room, expensively decorated and old-fashioned. We can tell it is raining outside — two men sit in armchairs:

First Man: "Ecrir une piece de theatre c'est de rendre aimable ceux que vous aimez le moins."

Second Man: "Oui?"

It was the world's shortest play. They had seen it before. Bollocks.

At home they have a conversation by the sofa.

MARY

Stop showing me your shirt you dirty great beast!

MIKE

You're very practical, darling.

MARY

You'd better believe it!

MIKE

What else have you got in the way of advice?

MARY

Avoid the divine. Like the plague. And boiling tar falling from the sky. And toads. I don't want you reading prayers to the moon every afternoon trying to get a tan. It won't do. OK?

MIKE

Gotcha. Prophets are a pain in the arse.

MARY

Mmm…

MIKE

I wish I'd been an architect.

MARY

So, what would have been your contribution to world architecture?

MIKE

More buildings should have some sort of cup on top.

(Mike feels Mary's bum.)

MARY

Stop feeling my bum, you hussy.

MIKE

My parents are being a bit weird at the moment. I'm really worried.

MARY

If your parents are getting divorced try and yawn with them.

MIKE

They're so old-fashioned.

MARY

The problem with parenting is the age difference.

MIKE

What about the holiday?

MARY

I've booked the flights.

MIKE

Ah! Those planes!

MARY

To call an aeroplane a great big flying moose is wrong. Don't do it.

MIKE

I'm bloody looking forward to this holiday!

MARY

Where are you going to put your virility?

MIKE

I'll put it with you.

MARY

I know, too. Now come on.

MIKE

Have you ever noticed how sometimes the sky is completely black?

MARY

What, no stars?

MIKE

And no city lights.

MARY

You'd have to be out in the country.

MIKE

Yes. That's what it's like. In here. In my head.

MARY

You're depressed.

MIKE

Yes.

MARY

You may be depressed but you're still . . . romantic.

MIKE

There's something missing. I hate it.

MARY

Don't attempt everything.

MIKE

I mean, what if we don't achieve what we want to achieve? Before we die. I swear, the music of the spheres is so powerful it can bite your head off.

MARY

The brain is a moral organ. Use it.

MIKE

How?

MARY

There are always revelations.

(PAUSE)

MIKE

Do other people have thoughts?

MARY

Yes, darling.

MIKE

Really?

MARY

It is my firm belief that everyone is essentially yummy. Just think about it. There are pretty attractive people everywhere. There are, indeed, completely perfect people virtually everywhere.

MIKE

It all seems so, sort of, angry.

MARY

Your subconscious is quicker than you.

(PAUSE)

MIKE

But I want to achieve everything. I want you, I want the world, I want everything. I don't want to die.

MARY

You won't remember dying.

MIKE

I'm lonely.

MARY

Eat some fruit. Achievement, old chap.

MIKE

I suppose.

MARY

What sort of person do you want to be admired by?

MIKE

I don't know.

MARY

Life is short. And long. Thank God.

MIKE

Well, thanks for spreading the mood!

MARY

It's your life. I hope the air is nutty for you.

MIKE

What does Mume say? "If life is circular, the problem is getting from A to B."

MARY

(Smiling) You're a bright star, honey.

MIKE

Are you afraid of death?

MARY

I'm not afraid of death. I like conclusions. If you know what the future brings, you're probably very sane.

MIKE

I know.

MARY

What came first, the ambition or the blank?

MIKE

That's a good question.

(PAUSE)

Can I put my collapsible rainbow into your full frontal flower box?

(PAUSE)

MARY
Alright.

They embrace.

CHAPTER 23: MARY GOES TO HOSPITAL

My understanding of the world
Is boundaried by pain.
Sometimes shafts of light or truth
Refresh like summer rain.

My body's fed and tutored well,
A place from which to be.
Do we do it for ourselves?
Or hope they'll follow me?

My mind, or thought, can sometimes feel
A joy that knows no space.
Eternity in orange peel
Or thoughts from mother's face.

Mary has to make an emergency visit to the hospital. The lighting down the corridor is nauseating. The nurse there deals with bumps to the head, bruises and, you know...ankles. They meet a small boy with bumps to the head.

"You're a fairy, aren't you?" says the small boy.

"You don't really want to be here, do you?" replies Mike.

" What should I do?"

"Pretend to be bored" replies the nurse.

Out in the corridor two male nurses are playing a game with wooden spatulas. They take it in turns.

"Say 'Ahh'".

"Ahh".

"Say 'Ahh'".

"Ahh".

Are they Sape and Werther, The Men In Dark Suits? Now Soap and Water.

"You prats," says Mike.

Mary comes home with Mike and a baby boy.

CHAPTER 24: WATCHING TELLY

The dictates of a poorly man
Are often blazed with light.
A second self that sees the plan
And's seasoned by the plight.

Blasted waves of ecstasy
Surface once again.
Simple words that make men see,
From the poorly pen.

"Transform suffering back to beauty,
Where it started out.
Life's a chamber fixed by duty,
Innocence and doubt."

More years having passed and Mary and Mike now have two children, a boy, 8 and a girl, 6. They watch the following television programme together as a family, *Sunny and Viv in the Bath*. Each week the two Clowns discuss their plans for revolution.

SUNNY

I've a terrific idea for a new shoe.

VIV

Have you? What is it?

SUNNY

Well, it involves getting bits of mattresses and sewing them all together.

VIV

You've tried doing that already, haven't you?

SUNNY

No. Yes. But now I've got some really good ideas.

VIV

And how do you think this will better our hopes for the future?

SUNNY

It's the way I'm seeing the world today. The scope and potential of shoes is gravely underrated.

VIV

What are these ideas?

SUNNY

I thought it would be a good idea to have a draw for putting things in. Actually in the shoe. In the heel or something. You could put thimbles or peanuts or buttons and things in it. I think it could be quite useful.

VIV

Who would want to carry things stored in their shoe?

SUNNY

Not necessarily those things, but I think it could be a good additional feature. Some extra incentive to buy them.

VIV

Do you think people will want to carry around thimbles and things tucked into their heels.

SUNNY

Absolutely.

VIV

And helium. If you have a space in the shoe for helium, you could make the shoe lighter. You could make the soles really huge, and then you'd be able to store heavy things in the sole. And possibly, if there was enough helium, the shoes wouldn't actually weigh anything at all.

SUNNY

You'd have to tie them down. Or you could put neon in the shoes and have glowing, cushion soles.

A baby girl and small boy are being helped in a bath

VIV

You're planning to abolish footwear altogether aren't you, Sunny?

SUNNY

That's right, Vivian.

VIV

Don't you think that might be quite difficult?

SUNNY

Not at all.

VIV

What with virtually everyone in the country owning at least one pair. Some people owning twenty-five pairs.

SUNNY

No. I don't think so. I think it's quite a reasonable idea.

VIV

How do you think you can do it?

SUNNY

Well. I know it's not going to be easy to rid the entire nation of all forms of footwear, but there is a way.

VIV

Please do tell.

SUNNY

What we have to do first is increase the general interest in shoes. It will have to start small and gradually increase, but I've got it all worked out. We have to make people care more about shoes first.

VIV

And that will lead to their demise? People care about shoes quite a lot.

SUNNY

We have to make them better. We have to generate a craze for footwear that we alone will mastermind. It's a question of building up the scale of things. First of all we have to monopolise the shoe industry.

VIV

That shouldn't be too tricky.

SUNNY

Exactly. I've got a few contacts. Make a few calls. Ring a few bells

VIV

But have you actually designed any shoes yet?

SUNNY

Yes. I've done a lot of work already and have some fabulous plans for the new era in footwear.

VIV

The last era in footwear.

SUNNY

Ever.

VIV

In the history of the earth.

SUNNY
Yes.
VIV
Blimey.
SUNNY
Are you in?
VIV
Yes.

Small girl talks for the first time

VIV
So tell me, how will making shoes better lead to their demise?
SUNNY
What we have to do is get everybody addicted to them. To do that we have to make them really good.

And then once they're addicted, we make them bigger and better. We turn the addiction into fanaticism, we turn the fanaticism into obsession and eventually the obsession will turn into hysteria. At the same time we have to increase the appeal of the shoe in greater and greater measures. We do this by exaggerating them in every respect. Slowly at first and then adding more and more things. More gadgets, more options; we make them slicker, slacker, bolder, bouncier, better and bigger. What we will actually be doing is making them worse. Monstrous. But they won't realise it, so drugged will they be by the shoes. As the shoes become more and more ridiculous, so will the addiction, until the opiate fever will reach such pitch that the momentum will burst outwards and at last, with a gigantic implosion, people will see their mistake. Shoes will have reached such absurd proportions, such foul propensity, such monstrous decadence, that it will result in nothing less than a revolution. Their horror at themselves will be absolute and shoes will be banned. Shoes will be made a thing of the past.

VIV

So, have you had any first thoughts about how to get the ball rolling? Unless people reject shoes of their own free will it won't be a proper and complete revolution.

SUNNY

Yes. We can't have pockets of resistance. What if there are people who aren't enumerated to the new concept in shoes?

VIV

Or if people start outlawing them before the rest of the nation has clicked?

SUNNY

There will have to be blanket coverage.

VIV

Consensus

SUNNY

Right.

VIV

But how can we do that?

SUNNY

We must get the help of shoes.

VIV

But how can we do that?

SUNNY

We will build them!

Young boy writes his first words

SUNNY

I've done a bit of research. Now, anything that is well designed and trained and with the right materials can gain intelligence. It just depends on the complexity. The more complex we make the shoes the brainier they will become. We will have to train them, so we'll need their co-operation. They will have a form of conscious-ness so we'll need to tell them what they have to do.

VIV

But not to tell them that they will eventually be killed off.

SUNNY

Exactly. It's unlikely we'll be able to get them to breed but that is to our advantage. After all, we wouldn't want them to take over the earth!

VIV

No.

SUNNY

It's all got to do with stealth. When a pair of shoes has stealth, that's when it's doing nothing. That's when they'll be communicating with each other.

VIV

In their subversive way.

SUNNY

What?

VIV

In their subversive way!

SUNNY

Yes. She shoes themselves will breed the hysteria. The spore-like lattices of their odours will enable a fungus-like language to develop. And these communications will be the key to the maintenance and stability of shoe mania. Now these stealth moments happen most when people are standing around chatting. So if we can get as many people standing around in bars it will give the shoes an opportunity to chat amongst themselves and promulgate the myth.

VIV

What?

SUNNY

Promulgate the myth!

VIV

Right.

Little boy goes to the loo by himself

VIV

Do you think the shoes will try and lick themselves? Well, they have tongues, don't they?

SUNNY

Yes, that could be a problem. Some of the shoes might want to break free and run off somewhere and start a nursery or something and teach smaller shoes. But fortunately shoes can't actually walk unless there's somebody actually in them. So we're alright there.

VIV

That's good.

SUNNY

Yes.

Girl reads book for first time

SUNNY

It's going very well. In Peterborough they're wearing shoes the size of walruses. Made of walrus. They look like walruses. Being worn by walruses.

VIV

So what's next?

SUNNY

I've been working on a new grip. This grip will be so good sometimes you'll wear the shoes and want to wet yourself. The kind of grip that grips so hard sometimes it will be difficult to stand in an empty garage in them without wanting to sprint.

VIV

To sprint like a rubber machine.

SUNNY

Exactly. I've got some new patterns being sent over from a friend in Norway. And one in Portugal. And one in Italy. I haven't told them yet but I'm going to combine the three best grip patterns on earth to produce the best grip pattern on earth.

VIV

Will it be better than the original ones?

SUNNY

What, the Norway, Portugal, Italy ones?

VIV

Yes.

SUNNY

Probably.

VIV

Blimey!

SUNNY

The secret is to combine them on the computer to produce one of those Magic Eye patterns. When someone's wearing the shoes the ground or mat or whatever they're standing on will read the grip. Not every surface can read very well so the grip has to be designed very accurately so even the most basic of dusty tracks will be able to read the grip pattern on the bottom of the shoe.

VIV

The research for discovering the reading capability of floors and roads is astonishingly labour intensive isn't it? Actually discovering a common language for every surface in the land that can be trodden on. It must have taken a while.

SUNNY

Yes, it did take a while. I had some help from the guys at the Met Office. They know an awful lot about the absorption of rain into organic surfaces and the patterns produced by drainage on a wide range of tarmacs and stone surfaces. It all leads to an understanding of the common earth in its ability to relate to those walking on it.

VIV

Now you have an understanding of the reading habits of solid ground, how does that make the shoes grip better?

SUNNY

The ground will be lulled.

VIV

Mmm. I should say.

SUNNY

A bond will form. A one sided attachment. The conscience of the beneath will draw interest from the shoe, dispelling any other thoughts it may have been having. The nature of the brief contact will have the surface sucking up for more. The curious flippant nature of the sole. The bashful obsessiveness of its charm. The pastiche of shape and form. The decisive flux of a vision. The lure of unpredictable contact. All this will increase the grip. The ground will actually swell up to greet the next step, each step a moon of instantaneous satisfaction to pace. The shoe will always have the upper hand. The ground will be left breathless. In exactly the same position it was in before. Panting. Craving contact. Anything. A cling so latent and depraved the ground won't know what's hit it. By this time the shoe will have disappeared, ruthless in its pursuit. Uncomprehended, further and further away, lapping the ground for more and quicker attention. A pan of diversion. Quicker than a transatlantic udder. Uncomprehending in its haste.

Boy ties shoelace for first time

VIV
Will your shoes have laces?
SUNNY
The laces will be shiny. The shiny laces will unhook people into an opium of carefulness. Lace technology is fast and this may be the way forwards. There will even be spare laces. Each shoe will be shiny, will bring brilliance to the feet and shall twinkle with light and lumus, and shall have a life raft. Each shoe will have several, maybe a dozen life rafts. And all the shoes

must have a lighthouse. Each of them must have beacons. Many beacons. Decorations of sand and outward beams of colossal brightness and clear multivitamined turquoise and orange and red and blue light. Each shoe must be equipped for a flood.

VIV

What about velcro?

SUNNY

Yes. And straps. Straps on the tips for unusual circumstances and straps on the side in case of collisions with skirting boards or shop fronts.

VIV

Will there be eyelets?

SUNNY

There will be eyelets for each day of the week. This shoe will have a drinks cabinet, a chiller and an ice machine.

VIV

No doubt there will be stripes on it?

SUNNY

These stripes will be taken from an idea grown naturally from the hedge-rows of the Middle Ages. Born through the ages by fruit. A timeless, side of the road idea. Honed countless times by the scents of local farmyard matures and passing fishermen. A rare but essential ingredient in the nourishment of any good idea.

The kind of idea only rustic briars and thorns can manipulate into existence. Changed and matured over centuries. Made animal, made wild and plucked again into the human realm. The kind of idea that changes ownership a thousand times before anyone knows it's an idea. It gathers and multiplies in intricacy a thousand time simpler in each unfolding. Through airs, touched by humans unknown and untouched by humans known. Brushed by animals and lived in through nests and holes. Stolen from by birds, hounded by squirrels and made mighty in loneliness prolonged by silences. The stripe will then be transported to America where especially trained scientists will be able to make it faster. It will then be transported back to me by the quickest means available and should arrive on my desk by email at about four o'clock tomorrow afternoon.

VIV

Trousers, Sunny. If the project's really going to work they're going to have to interact with trousers.

SUNNY

That shouldn't be a problem. A lot of them get on very well already. Some of them need introductions but the smart shoes have a way of getting trousers over to their side. In fact the shoes are getting closer to the psyche of many and faster and that is as a direct resulty of their worky with the trousers.

Girl rides bike for first time

VIV
Toes.
SUNNY
Yes. Toes. The toenail is misunderstood in these isles. In Scandinavia toenails are harvested and secretly put into unusual ovens to expand them and make them into roofing tiles. They are then disguised with a particular industrial nail varnish that contains beer to prevent people in the suburbs from getting suspicious. There are fields of people growing toenails in this fashion. Hundreds of perfectly trained Scandinavians are happily taking time off their family lives to lie around in meadows with their socks off, having their toes massaged by drugged butterflies. The butterflies tickle the toes to extend the growing process with the assistance of ointments. I think that's something we should be thinking about in this country. We may be able to gain some kind of foothold. A grip. Some sort of shoe in. It could be a heel. A step in the right direc-

tion. One foot first, then the next. We could nail this one. It could be sole destroying at first. It might get a bit hairy.

VIV

Just think what the future holds.

SUNNY

What we need to think about is the relation of buildings to shoes. The absence of shoes to toes, but importantly, of toenails to buildings. There is a link here that must be unfolded. What connects a mountain lodge, a velcro ceiling and a bare footed nail festival is anyone's guess but when shoes are abolished, things will change. It will be as if a new sky is opening in opposing directions. When shoes have become so large and have been banished there will be a rebirth of the toenail. A discovery of lines inexistent before. People will move rapidly over vast plains of grass, their feet brushing their ears in voluminous sweeping rotations. It could even signify the age of the knee. Congregations will occur. Onions will be freely talked about. Heels and bunions will be uprooted from their torture and misery. It's highly likely there will be new age of ballet. The technology of paddling may be brought forward to new and greater forms of sophistication. At the moment there is nobody but amateurs in the science of paddling. Ballet and paddling. Many will be the congregations of ballet paddlers in huge new shallow waters. There will be new vast areas dedicated to shallow bathing of all sorts. Some with mud. Some with scents and disinfectants. Others a mighty homage to clean water. Some with pebbles, others with sand.

VIV

What will become of the shoe?

SUNNY

Great sculptures will be made. Huge floating mono-liths. Paths will be constructed from upturned shoes. There will be meadows constructed from the remains of shoe. Great forests will be dedicated to the memory of past footwear. There will be towns made of shoe and shoes that lean. Roads will be a thing of the past and architecture itself may indeed dissolve. Great rows of shoes will be constructed. Acres of fields with shoes pointing to the sky. Unfoldable mountain ranges with comfortable walking surfaces will be constructed.

VIV

The landmass itself will become the universal shoe.

SUNNY

I can't wait.

VIV

Nnn.

SUNNY

Time for bed now, wouldn't you say?

VIV

I think you're right.

SUNNY

OK.

VIV

Right then.

SUNNY

Goodnight Viv.

VIV

Goodnight Sunny.

SUNNY

Have you shut the hens up?

VIV

Oh! No.

SUNNY

I'll do it, then.

VIV

Oh! Thanks!

SUNNY

You know, the ground. It might be a bit . . . pointy.

VIV

Mmm.

SUNNY

Have we still got those wellies?

VIV

Yes, I think so.

SUNNY

I think I'll put them on before I go outside.

VIV

You think so?

SUNNY

I think it would be best.

VIV

Praps you're right.

SUNNY

OK, Viv.

Mike takes the remote control and switches off the telly.

"This is how I see it," he says.

He pauses and looks up. Continues.

"Let us wear boomerangs on our person. For they come back."

"Let us not overcook cabbage. Lest we forget."

"Let us wear black if we are wheels. Because we are grippers."

"Let us not underestimate brooms. For they are more hairy."

"Let umbrellas talk to each other. It is rainy."

"Let us call fences hedges and hedges fences. For they are much the same."

"Let shoes be slidey. For we walk in them."

Pause.

"For what we have received."

"Barmen."

Mike and Mary slowly get up and leave the room.

The son, 8 on sofa, grabs the remote and turns on the telly. It blares at him and his sister. A creepy reminder of Hero with its adverts for bodily functions and everything. A few moments pass.

THE SON BELCHES LOUDLY.

His sister 6, HITS HIM ON THE ARM.

"Stop it!" she howls.

BACK TO THE TELLY.

THEY WATCH.

FADE OUT.

THE END